Marketing Plan

Realestaternator™

by George Peter Gatsis

HERITAGE HOUSE
FOR SALE!

6 Bedrooms, 8½ Bathrooms, 2 Kitchens, Study, Huge Backyard, Original Fixtures, Walk-in Closets, Fire Place, Classic Lighting, Washer & Dryer, Slightly Haunted, Library, Hard Wood Flooring, Large Oak Trees Quiet Neighbourhood, 2 Stories + Attic.

BEST OFFER
MOVE IN IMMEDIATELY!

THE BLACK DIAMOND EFFECT® ....Volume 1, No. 55
REALESTATERNATOR

Critical Blast Publishing
624 Sunnyhill Drive
Belleville, IL 62223

Edited by R.J. Carter.

First Edition Dec 2025

0 9 8 7 6 5 4 3 2 1

ISBN: 978-1-998564-57-6 — Digest

Distributed by Critical Blast Logistics - CriticalBlast.com / PRINTED IN USA.

Court House: The Case

Gavel Falls

The air in Room 17 of the old county courthouse hung thick with the smell of polished oak, stale coffee, and the faint metallic tang of tension. It was a Friday morning in late spring, and the high windows let in pale shafts of sunlight that caught the drifting dust like slow-motion snow. Only a handful of spectators dotted the worn public benches (retirees with nothing better to do, a couple of off-duty cops nursing hangovers, and one man who looked as if he had stepped straight out of a 1973 disco).

Joe "Joey Knuckles" Moretti leaned against the back wall in a plaid sport coat so loud it could wake the dead. The jacket was two sizes too big, the trousers two inches too short, and the whole ensemble screamed "I bought this the day after Studio 54 closed and never looked back." A wad of Bazooka gum worked steadily in his cheek while his dark eyes, half-lidded with practiced boredom, never left the front of the room.

Up at the bar stood Skip Hargrove, a man built like a coat hanger in a navy suit that had once been expensive. His Adam's apple bobbed above a tie the color of dishwater, and his fingers worried the knot as though it might strangle him before the morning was out. Beside him, tall, cool, and unflappable, stood Cynthia Langford, the city's assistant solicitor. Blonde hair pulled back in a severe bun, charcoal skirt suit tailored sharp enough to draw blood, eyes the pale blue of glacier ice. She shuffled papers with the calm of a card shark who already knew the river card.

Judge Harlan Smith presided from the bench like a tired lion who had seen every trick in the savanna. His black robe hung loose on a frame that had once been imposing; now the years had whittled him down to gristle and gravel. He peered over half-moon glasses at the nervous man before him.

"Okay, Skip," the judge rumbled, voice dry as November leaves. "I can call you Skip, I think. This is the tenth time I've had you in here in six days. I'm starting to feel we should have adjoining parking spaces."

A nervous chuckle rippled through the gallery. Skip managed a sickly nod. "Yes, sir."

Judge Smith flipped through the petition. "What we have here is a request to demolish the structure at 32 Mount Triplet Road. Your property, correct?"

"Yes, sir."

The judge turned to Cynthia. "Counselor Langford, any reason I shouldn't grant this perfectly reasonable request from a man who clearly loves paperwork?"

Cynthia's smile was thin and professional. "Several, Your Honor."

Skip's head snapped toward her so fast something in his neck cracked. "Wait—who are you?"

"Skip," the judge warned, "you will address the court, not the city solicitor."

Skip blinked, confused. "You're not the coffee girl?"

A ripple of laughter. Even Joe in the back row snorted gum into his sinus.

Cynthia stepped forward and handed the judge a thick folder. "Your Honor, the house at 32 Mount Triplet Road was officially designated a heritage structure by city ordinance 14-B last year. It is the oldest standing residence in the city limits—built in 1871 as the original surveyor's cottage and used as the model for the first wave of settler homes. Every other house from that period has long since been demolished or burned. This is the last one."

Skip stared at the documents sliding across the bench like they were written in Aramaic. "Wait—what!?"

The judge leafed through faded sepia photographs: a lone clapboard house surrounded by open wheat fields, a hand-painted sign reading MOUNT TRIPLET LAND OFFICE, 1871. He gave a low whistle. "Well, I'll be damned. This is a wrench the size of Texas, Miss Langford."

He looked down at Skip, who was still trying to parse the legalese. "Counselor Hargrove?"

Skip exploded. "This is bullshit!"

The gavel cracked like a gunshot. "Language, Mr. Hargrove! I will not have a sewer mouth in my courtroom."

Skip swallowed hard. "I—I beg the court's forgiveness, Your Honor. But if I can't renovate or tear the place down, I can't sell it—"

"—for the obscene profit you were counting on," Cynthia finished smoothly.

Skip wheeled on her. "Lady, are you sure your true calling isn't fetching lattes?"

"Quite sure," she replied, ice crackling in her voice.

"It's a boring, plain, falling-apart old shack! It has zero tourist value. I'd go broke just printing the brochures. Who the hell wants to pay money to see a broken-down, raggedy old house?"

Judge Smith leaned forward, elbows on the bench. "Then I guess you'll sell it at cost. Or eat the loss. Either way, that house stays exactly as it is. Request denied."

The gavel fell again—final as a coffin lid.

Cynthia gathered her files with calm precision. Skip stalked past her toward the aisle.

He leaned in, voice a venomous hiss. "Bitch. I'll have that Cracker Jack law license revoked before lunch."

"You have a wonderful day, too, Mr. Hargrove," she answered sweetly.

She tapped a manicured finger against her chin, eyes glittering. "Though you might want to worry less about my license and more about someone discovering you talked a dying old woman into signing over her childhood home while she was doped to the gills on morphine."

Skip froze. "She signed it fair and square."

"That's not the version I hear around the water cooler."

"Hearing and proving are two very different things, sweetheart."

Cynthia's smile never wavered. "Your client died, and twenty-four hours later you're in here trying to flip her house for six figures. People are talking, Skip."

"You can't prove a thing, you tramp."

"Have a great day," she repeated, turning on her heel and gliding out.

Skip stood fuming, then affected an exaggerated imitation of her poised walk, rolling his papers into a tube and stuffing them into his breast pocket. The jacket bulged like he'd concealed a small squirrel.

He was almost to the doors when a meaty hand clamped onto his shoulder.

"Hey, howya doin', Realestaternator," Joey Knuckles Moretti said, chomping gum like it owed him money. Up close he smelled of Aqua Velva and cigarette smoke baked into polyester. "The boss sends his regards." His voice dropped to a confidential murmur. "And a friendly reminder."

Skip tried to shrug him off. Joey's grip tightened.

"You got till end of the week to deliver the envelope, Skippy."

"Or what?"

Joey glanced theatrically left and right, then leaned in until Skip could count the gold caps on his molars. "Or you're dead."

"If you kill me you don't get your money!"

"Then your family's dead."

"I don't have a family."

"Your friends, then."

"I live alone."

"Your parents catch a bullet."

"They've been dead ten years."

Joey's grin widened, shark-like. "Then we dig the bastards up and shoot 'em again! Capeesh? You don't wanna find out how creative the boss gets when he's disappointed."

Skip swallowed. "What if I just sign the house over to your boss? Clean title, problem solved."

Joey barked a laugh that turned heads. "What are we, Century 21? Paper trail goes to the city clerk, clerk runs the name, IRS crawls so far up the boss's ass he'll need a colonoscopy and a tax attorney. Cash, Skip. Cold, hard, untraceable cash. The boss don't want real estate—he wants the green."

Skip opened his mouth, closed it.

"And don't think about skipping town," Joey continued, straightening Skip's crooked tie with mock gentleness. "We got a very special person watching you. Real close. Like, shares-your-toothbrush close."

The two men locked eyes—predator and prey in cheap suits.

"Look, pal," Joey said, almost kindly, "you bet on the wrong horse, you lost big. Time to pay the vigorish. Capeesh?"

Skip watched Joey Knuckles saunter away, plaid jacket flashing like a warning beacon. Only when the doors swung shut did he realize his hands were shaking.

He drew a ragged breath, smoothed his lapels, and stepped out into the bright, indifferent morning—knowing full well that somewhere out there, eyes were already on him.

Monday Morning
Selling the House:
CLIENT 01

First Showing

Monday morning on Mount Triplet Road, and the sun was already doing its best to bake the cracked asphalt. The house at number 32 crouched at the end of a cul-de-sac like a tired old dog that refused to die. Peeling white paint, sagging gutters, a widow's walk that leaned five degrees off true; everything about it screamed money pit. Yet there it stood, stubbornly historic, stubbornly unsellable.

Skip Hargrove waited on the porch, hands trembling just enough that the keys jingled like cheap wind chimes. He'd popped two antacids on the drive over and still tasted copper. A shiny red Prius pulled up, and out stepped the brightest-eyed newlyweds this side of a jewelry commercial: Ethan and Madison Parker, both twenty-six, both still believing love conquered closing costs.

Ethan wore the earnest grin of a man who'd never met a mortgage he couldn't sweet-talk. Madison clutched his arm like he was the last life jacket on the Titanic, her ponytail bouncing with every excited step.

Skip forced his salesman smile until it hurt. "Price is honestly a steal for the location," he began, voice cracking only once. "Two blocks from the light-rail, four-minute walk to Northgate Mall—"

Madison squealed before he finished the sentence. Ethan kissed her temple, and together they bounded up the steps. Skip fumbled the key twice, then pushed the door open on hinges that groaned like a dying moose.

Inside, the foyer smelled of dust and something faintly metallic. Sunlight slanted through grimy windows and painted long rectangles across scarred oak floors.

"Aren't you coming in?" Ethan asked.

Skip planted himself in the doorway, one foot in, one foot out, as if crossing the threshold fully might be legally binding. "Nope. You two lovebirds go right ahead. Take it all in. Savor the possibilities."

Madison giggled and darted toward the kitchen. Ethan took the stairs two at a time, calling, "Gonna check the bedrooms!"

Skip stayed put, leaning against the jamb, counting heartbeats.

Down the short hallway, Madison flung open drawers and cupboards with the glee of a kid on Christmas. The cutlery rattled like bones. She pulled out a serving fork the length of a Roman gladius and laughed. "Ethan, honey, look at these! We could host Thanksgiving for the entire National Guard!"

Upstairs, Ethan ran appreciative hands over the master bedroom's dark walnut woodwork. The bed frame was heavy Victorian, carved with grapes and gargoyles. From the en-suite came the unmistakable hiss of a shower.

"Hello?" Ethan calledafely. "Anybody there?"

The bathroom door stood ajar, steam curling out like cigarette smoke. He nudged it wider.

A woman stepped from the mist—naked, raven-haired, maybe thirty, skin still glistening. She smiled with lazy confidence and extended one hand.

"Hand me a towel, handsome?"

Ethan's brain short-circuited. The woman was stunning: high cheekbones, full lips, curves that belonged on a museum wall. He fumbled for the thick terry-cloth towel on the rack.

"What... what are you doing here?" he managed.

She tilted her head, water dripping from dark curls. "Silly boy. I don't want the big towel." She pointed to a hand towel no larger than a dinner napkin. "The little one."

Ethan glanced at it, baffled. "That won't even—"

She closed the distance, trailing wet footprints across the tile. Her fingers brushed his cheek, cool and deliberate. "Tell me, are you married?"

"Yes," he croaked, then louder, "Yes, just this weekend, actually."

Her laugh was low, delighted. "Perfect. I adore married

men. All that delicious danger." She leaned closer, breath warm against his ear. "Especially when the wife is downstairs admiring the Sub-Zero."

Ethan's gaze flicked toward the bedroom. Somewhere below, Madison was still cooing over vintage cabinetry.

"We'd have to be quick," the woman whispered, "but I promise you've never felt anything like—"

The door banged wide. Madison stood frozen on the threshold, eyes huge.

"What are you doing!?"

Ethan spun, arms flailing. "Maddie, no—it's not—"

The naked woman seized Ethan's shoulders and yanked him against her. In the space of a heartbeat her beauty melted away like candle wax. Skin sagged, hair thinned to gray wisps, eyes sank into nests of wrinkles. What had been a siren was now a crone, naked and grinning with yellowed teeth.

"Back to the vibrator for you, sweetheart," the old woman rasped at Madison. "This one's mine."

Madison screamed—one high, piercing note that could shatter crystal—and bolted.

Ethan stared in horror as the hag's fingers dug between her own sagging breasts. With a wet, ripping sound she tore open her rib cage like a coat. Inside was not flesh but darkness, writhing, hungry. Organs the color of spoiled plums slithered out and hit the tile with wet slaps, inching toward Ethan on pulsing ropes of intestine.

He found his legs at last and fled, nearly tumbling down the stairs.

In the foyer Skip watched Madison burst out the front door, ponytail whipping like a battle standard. Ethan followed half a second later, face the color of skim milk.

Skip's salesman reflex kicked in. "We have an excellent house-warming package—"

Both newlyweds sprinted past him.

"I'll knock ten percent off asking!"

Car doors slammed. The Prius fishtailed down the street, Madison's voice floating back through the open window: "How could you!"

Skip cupped hands around his mouth. "Free satellite for a year! HBO! Cinemax! All the channels!"

Tires squealed. They were gone.

Skip exhaled, shoulders sagging. He turned back to the house.

Something vast and lightless oozed down the staircase, a living shadow thicker than smoke. It pooled at the threshold, blotting out the sunlight rectangle by rectangle until the doorway was nothing but a slab of black.

The front door slammed in Skip's face hard enough to rattle the stained-glass pane.

He stumbled backward down the porch steps, nearly tripping over his own feet. When he looked up again, the darkness was already receding, soaking back into the walls like ink into blotter paper, leaving only the faint smell of ozone and old blood.

Skip stood alone on the dying lawn, the **FOR SALE** sign creaking in the breeze.

He rubbed the back of his neck, stared at the innocent-looking house, and muttered the only thing that felt appropriate.

"Well… crap."

Monday Noon
Selling the House:
Client ☆02

Three Strikes, Still Breathing

Monday had turned into a slow-motion car crash, and the house at 32 Mount Triplet Road was the immovable object in the middle of the intersection.

Hard Sale

The front door creaked open again and the Patel clan poured in like a colorful, noisy river: Rajesh Patel, patriarch and proud grandfather of six; his wife Anjali, sari the color of ripe mango; and the grandchildren themselves, ages three to twelve, already treating the foyer like a racetrack. Shoes flew off in every direction, tiny feet thundered across the oak floor, and the air filled with the high-pitched symphony of sugar-fueled chaos.

Rajesh, thickset and dignified, silver mustache bristling, planted himself in front of Skip. "You list house for sale," he declared in a rolling Bombay baritone, "yet clearly you cannot sell. I will buy, but you will come down. Now."

Skip opened his mouth. Rajesh raised one finger, the universal sign for silence. "Tut-tut-tut. No excuses. I have many mouths. Thirty-five percent off, minimum."

Skip swallowed. "Sir, I've already shaved the price to the bone—"

"Grandchildren," Rajesh corrected, gesturing at the whirlwind of kids. "Their lazy parents are at work. I feed them all. Thirty-five percent."

Before Skip could answer, the grandchildren shrieked past like a flock of starlings, nearly bowling him over. Rajesh barked something in Gujarati that translated roughly to "Behave or no ice cream for a month!"

Anjali Patel swept in, eyes blazing. Without warning her palm cracked across Skip's cheek hard enough to rattle teeth.

"This house is haunted!" she announced to her husband, as if Skip were simply furniture. "You are the man of the house and I obey always, but if you buy this cursed place I stop cooking. No more roti, no aloo gobi, no butter chicken. Nothing. You will starve, husband."

She rounded on Skip, wagging a finger thick with gold rings. "And you! Shame on you. The things she told me about you upstairs. Very bad man. Very, very bad."

Anjali stormed out. Behind her, the darkness began pooling at the edge of the foyer like spilled oil.

Skip rubbed his stinging cheek. "Fifteen percent off?" he offered weakly.

Rajesh shook his head sadly. "Ghost. No deal."

"Twenty?"

"You ask me to give up sweet-potato roti cooked in white wine and cumin? Never." He joined his wife on the porch. The door slammed so hard the stained glass rattled.

From the driveway came Anjali's satisfied voice: "Wise decision, dear. That is why you wear the pants."

Vic The Blade

Skip's face still throbbed when the next prospect arrived: Victor "Vic the Blade" Moreau, ex-Special Forces turned corporate security consultant. Six-four, built like a refrigerator in a charcoal Brioni suit, cigar the size of a rolling pin clenched between perfect teeth. He stepped out of a black Hummer that looked capable of invading small countries.

"As-is," Skip said before Vic even crossed the threshold. "Some lights in the basement are… temperamental."

Vic dropped a bulging olive-drab duffel, checked a tactical watch. "Listing says this place hit the market today."

"That's correct."

Vic grinned around the cigar, opened the bag, and lifted out a pair of military-grade night-vision goggles. "Always travel prepared."

3—4

Skip eyed the bag. "Planning to renovate the plumbing?"

"Wet work," Vic answered cheerfully.

"You kill people for money now?"

"Lots," Vic said, like a man discussing golf handicaps. "Stopped counting medals after mission one-hundred. Hand-to-hand, jungle, desert, urban—you name it. Toughest sonofabitch you'll ever meet. Don't tell the wife, the girlfriend, or the mistress."

He laughed at his own joke, strode deeper into the foyer, and slipped on the goggles. "Needs paint at the very least—"

A bony hand shot from nowhere, clamped around Vic's thick neck, and slammed him against the wallpaper hard enough to crack the lath beneath. The cigar flew from his lips.

The old woman from the bathroom—now dressed in a tattered housecoat the color of dried blood—pressed a twelve-inch carving knife to Vic's cheek. Her voice was a graveyard whisper.

"Touch one inch of my house and I'll gut you stem to stern. You won't have time to bleed—you'll be too busy shitting your intestines into your boots."

She released him and simply wasn't there anymore.

Vic stumbled backward, caught his heel on the runner rug, and crash-landed on his pride. He scrambled out the door on all fours, dignity shredded.

Skip watched from the porch, resigned. "Seriously?"

The duffel bag and goggles came sailing through the air like angry luggage, landing on the grass with twin thuds. The door slammed again—final, absolute.

Vic peeled out in the Hummer without a backward glance.

Skip stared at the abandoned gear, then at the house. The windows stared back, black and empty.

"If I make it to Friday," he said to no one, "no more sure bets. No more 'one last score.' I swear on every loan shark in the county."

He nudged the duffel with his shoe, half expecting it to explode.

The house said nothing. But somewhere inside, something old and patient waited for the next fool to cross the threshold.

MONDAY EVENING
THE GANG

Alley Entrepreneurs

Monday evening, and the alley behind the shuttered pawn shop smelled of stale beer, weed, and broken dreams. A single flickering streetlamp painted everything the color of old mustard. Seven young men lounged against graffiti-tagged brick like they owned the night, which, in this zip code, they sort of did.

Rocky Delgado, twenty-three going on forty, lean as a switchblade, hair slicked back with yesterday's pomade, stood at the center of the loose circle. His lieutenants ringed him: Lefty Vasquez combing his pride-and-joy pompadour every twelve seconds; Smokes Nguyen chain-smoking unfiltered Camels; Porkchop Moretti, no relation to Joey Knuckles, thank God, built like a vending machine with legs; Gamer Park hunched over a glowing Nintendo Switch; Mushi-Soshi Tanaka cracking his knuckles in perfect 4/4 time; and Numbers Washington, skinny, bespectacled, already doing mental math on their collective negative net worth.

Rocky sighed the sigh of a general whose army had run out of bullets and morale. "Another day, boys, and we still broker than a glass jaw."

Mushi-Soshi shrugged. "What can we do, boss?"

"Imports took all the good corners," Rocky said. "Koreans got the weed, Russians got the pills, Salvadorans got the protection. Hell, even the Armenians got the car-window wash hustle now."

Numbers pushed his glasses up. "Rob a liquor store?"

Rocky snorted. "You want HD footage of your dumb ass on WorldStar by sunrise? Every grandma's got a Ring camera now. By the time we hit the curb, drones'll be reading us our rights."

Porkchop rubbed his considerable belly. "We could, like… open a business or something."

"With what, Porky? We ain't got enough pooled to buy one taco, let alone a truck."

Rocky pinched the bridge of his nose. "I'm forced to a hard decision, fellas. I'm selling some of you to medical testing. Phase-one trials pay five grand easy."

A chorus of protests erupted. Gamer didn't even look up from his Switch. "Touch me and I'll 360-no-scope your kneecaps, ese."

"Relax, relax," Rocky said, hands raised. "It's for the greater good. Food. Rent. A clubhouse that isn't Porkchop's mom's basement. One day we'll be kings, but first we need a high-concept score that prints money fast."

Seven heads nodded solemnly.

Rocky spun dramatically and pointed down the alley like he'd rehearsed it. "And there, gentlemen, walks opportunity in a cheap suit."

Skip Hargrove appeared under the streetlamp looking like a man who'd lost a fight with his own reflection. Tie askew, eyes bloodshot, hands still trembling from the day's supernatural customer-service disasters.

The Vipers, self-proclaimed, though their logo was still only sharpied on one denim vest, closed around him like wolves who'd skipped lunch.

Lefty's switchblade comb flashed. Smokes blew a smoke ring in Skip's face. Porkchop cracked knuckles the size of walnuts.

Lefty slid practiced fingers into Skip's jacket and came out with a wallet thinner than communion wafer. He flipped it open, frowned. "Empty, boss. Dude's got terminal sickness."

"Terminal," Skip corrected weakly.

Rocky took the wallet, sniffed it like it might still have money smell. "What are you, an English teacher?"

"No. Why?"

"'Cause only two kinds of people walk into Viper Alley this calm: crazy or connected. Which are you?"

Skip raised both hands, palms out. "I need a house vacated."

Lefty grinned. "What we look like, doctors?"

"Vacated, not vaccinated," Skip said. "Old woman refuses to leave. Squatting in my listing."

Rocky's eyes narrowed. "You want us to put hands on a grandma? We got rules, man. No kids, no old folks."

"She's rich," Skip said.

The alley went still. Even Gamer paused his game.

Rocky leaned in. "Define rich."

"Rich enough to tie me up with lawyers for years. Never leaves the house. Pays every delivery in crisp hundreds. Mattress money. Shoebox money. Coffee-can money."

Numbers' head snapped up; dollar signs practically reflected in his glasses.

Rocky rubbed his chin. "Even if we ghost in at 3 a.m., somebody's Ring'll catch us. Social Media. NextDoor. Cops'll be waiting with lattes."

Skip slowly reached into his coat and produced the military night-vision goggles Vic the Blade had abandoned on the lawn. Then he nudged the abandoned duffel bag forward with his shoe. "Generation-three tubes. No glow, no signature. Plus whatever Rambo left in the bag. Move like ghosts, see like cats."

Seven pairs of eyes went from the goggles to Skip and back to the goggles.

Rocky broke the silence with a slow, wolfish smile.

"Boys," he said, clapping Skip on the shoulder hard enough to stagger him, "I do believe Christmas came early."

MONDAY NIGHT
THE BREAK-IN

Night the Vipers Learned Respect

Monday night pressed against the windows of 32 Mount Triplet Road like a living thing, thick, humid, and hungry. The moon hung low and bloated, the color of old bone. Inside, the house waited.

The front door eased open without a creak (professional work). Five figures slipped in, moving in practiced silence: Rocky, Lefty, Smokes, Porkchop, and Numbers. Night-vision goggles turned their eyes into glowing green coins. No flashlights, no phones, no chatter. Just the soft scuff of sneakers on oak and the shared heartbeat of men about to get rich or get dead.

Rocky raised a fist. Split. Lefty and Numbers peeled off toward the basement stairs. Smokes and Porkchop ghosted upward. Rocky himself flowed into the living room, scanning shelves and shadows for anything that looked like it could hold a fortune.

Basement

The stairs sighed under Lefty's weight. At the bottom, the air tasted of damp stone and something coppery. Numbers, ever the scholar, reached for a light switch out of sheer habit.

Click.

Harsh fluorescent tubes flared to life.

Lefty hissed like a scalded cat. "What the hell, man! Kill it!"

"But I can't see—"

"Kill it now!"

Numbers flipped the switch again. Darkness swallowed them, but not before Lefty memorized the layout: rows of dusty pickled jars, an ancient wringer washer, a dressmaker's mannequin draped in yellowed lace, a squat iron safe beside the furnace, a wall of pegged tools glinting like surgical instruments.

Numbers stepped forward. "Okay, genius. Now what?"

"Safe first, college boy. Beside the mannequin."

Numbers turned. "What mannequin?"

The mannequin was gone.

Second Floor – Guest Bedroom

Smokes nudged the door with his shoulder. The room looked innocent enough: peeling rose wallpaper, a brass bed, moonlight striping the floorboards. Except for the old woman standing motionless in the far corner, face hidden in shadow.

Smokes had half a second to register her before she charged (impossibly fast, mouth open in a silent scream). The door slammed shut on its own.

Hallway

Porkchop spun. "Smokes?"

Nothing answered but the house breathing.

He tried the bathroom. Shower curtain drawn the full length of the tub. He yanked it back—empty porcelain. Turned to leave. Caught movement in the mirror.

The old woman stood in the dry tub, smiling like a grandmother about to offer cookies.

Porkchop whipped around. Tub still empty.

Mirror again: she was right behind him now, head tilted, eyes black as oil.

He bolted.

Back in the hallway he flung open the guest-bedroom door. Empty. "Smokes, this ain't funny!"

He stepped inside, checked behind the door. Clear. When he turned, Smokes stood in the hallway, motionless, mouth working soundlessly, toes six inches off the floor. Invisible fingers circled his thick neck.

Porkchop poked Smokes in the chest. No reaction. The fingers tightened, then vanished. Smokes remained hanging.

Porkchop looked up.

The old woman looked down. Reached.

Porkchop's switchblade flashed. He slashed empty air, stumbled, fell. Cold hands locked around his ankles and dragged him backward into a patch of darkness that hadn't been there a heartbeat earlier. His scream cut off like a record yanked off the needle.

Library – First Floor

Rocky ran reverent fingers along leather spines. One shelf looked wrong, books jutting unevenly. He pulled them out one by one. Behind the last volume, a pair of ancient eyes stared back.

Rocky yelped, tripped over a coffee table, goggles tumbling. When he looked up, the old woman stood three feet away, calm as Sunday dinner.

He scrambled for his pistol. "Don't move!"

She took a step.

"I said don't—"

Another step.

He fired. The bullet punched into a first-edition Dickens; dust and paper confetti exploded.

"Where's the money, abuela?"

"Money?" Her voice was soft, almost amused.

"Give it up or I swear—"

"We?" she asked sweetly. "Who's we?"

Rocky's shout echoed down empty halls. "Numbers! Porkchop! Lefty! Smokes! Move your asses!"

She drifted closer. "Oh, you mean your friends?"

Rocky backed up until the wall kissed his shoulder blades. "Stay back!"

"Me?" She spread arthritic hands. "I'm just an old woman. You have the gun."

The temperature plummeted twenty degrees. Rocky's breath plumed white.

"Last chance—"

She was simply gone.

Hallway

Rocky lunged out of the library to find his crew on the front lawn, waving frantically, mouths forming silent words. He couldn't hear them. Between him and the open door stretched a wall of living black, expanding like spilled ink.

He emptied the magazine into it. The darkness swallowed the muzzle flashes whole.

The front door slammed an inch from his nose.

Front Lawn

The four surviving Vipers watched the door seal itself. A heartbeat later Rocky stumbled out of thin air beside them, on his knees, lips blue with cold.

Lefty hauled him up. "Boss!"

Rocky's teeth chattered. "Why… the hell… did you leave me?"

"We didn't!" Numbers protested. "One second we're inside, next second we're out here freezing our nuts off!"

A sound like every door in the house slamming at once rolled across the lawn. The streetlamp flickered and died.

Rocky found his voice. "We are never speaking of this again. Not one word. Street finds out we got run off by a freaky old lady, we're finished. Capeesh?"

Another groan, deeper, older, rose from the foundation. Windows glowed red for one heartbeat.

They ran. Sneakers slapped pavement until the house was a bad memory behind them.

Across the Street

Skip Hargrove leaned against a lamppost, drawing on a cigarette that tasted like failure. The Vipers scattered into the night like startled pigeons.

He muttered, "Damn," and flicked ash onto the sidewalk.

A small figure skipped into the circle of light: a little girl in a faded sundress, maybe eight, pigtails bobbing.

Skip glanced down. "Little late for you to be out, sweetheart."

She looked up with eyes far too old for her face. "Message from the boss," she said in a voice like candy-coated razor blades. "End of the week. Or else."

She skipped away, humming.

Skip stared after her until the cigarette burned his fingers. "Ouch."

Inside the House
Third Bedroom, Second Floor

From the darkness of an empty room, the old woman watched Skip's taillights disappear down Mount Triplet Road.

Something moved behind her, something large, patient, and very, very hungry.

She turned, smiling a welcome only the dead could love.

MONDAY NIGHT
THE BREAK-IN
AFTERMATH
HOMES

Slow Elevator to Nowhere

The city's neon bled across Skip Hargrove's windshield as he crawled downtown, saxophone jazz oozing from the speakers like cheap bourbon. He passed the Vipers still sprinting full-tilt along the sidewalk, Rocky in the lead, Porkchop lumbering like a freight train with a busted wheel. Skip gave the horn a polite little toot. Rocky flipped him the bird without breaking stride.

Skip turned into the underground parking of the Sterling Towers, tires chirping on polished concrete. The garage was half-lit and echoing. He killed the engine, sat for a moment listening to the tick of cooling metal, then heard it: a soft scrape, like claws on cement.

He jerked around. Nothing.

A black cat shot out from under a BMW, gave him a green-eyed sneer, and vanished between pillars.

Skip exhaled a laugh that sounded more like a cough and headed for the elevator lobby.

Four people already waited under the harsh fluorescents.

- A waiter in a rumpled white shirt and black vest, bowtie undone.

- A young fitness woman in neon leggings and a sports bra, earbuds dangling.

- An old businessman in a three-piece suit two decades out of fashion, leaning on a cane.

- A middle-aged woman mechanic, grease still under her nails, coveralls half-zipped over a tank top, flipping through a dog-eared copy of Houses & Condos Monthly.

Skip hit the call button that was already glowing. The mechanic never looked up. "Wow. Why didn't any of us geniuses think of pressing the button?"

The waiter rolled his eyes. "Slowest elevator in the Western Hemisphere."

Skip glanced at the magazine. "House hunting?"

The mechanic turned a page with deliberate slowness. "You're just full of obvious tonight, aren't you?"

Ding. The doors wheezed open like an asthmatic walrus. They piled in.

Skip tried again. "I sell houses. Anything particular you're looking for?"

"Old," the mechanic said, still reading. "Cheap. Enough room for me and my girlfriend to grow herbs and rescue dogs."

Skip's salesman reflex kicked in before his brain could slam on the brakes. "You know the place on Mount Triplet Road? Number 32. Built 1871. Total fixer, but—"

The old businessman's cane clattered against the rail. "Number 32? That's the haunted one."

The waiter snorted. "Bro, everybody knows that house. My cousin's buddy went in on a dare and came out speaking in tongues."

"Pass," the fitness woman muttered, thumbing her phone.

The mechanic finally looked up, eyes narrowing. "You trying to unload a lemon on me, slick?"

"No, no," Skip backpedaled as the elevator lurched upward. "Just… it's old. Historic. Character."

The waiter leaned in. "Character like poltergeist character. Tell your client to burn it down and salt the earth."

Ding. Fourteenth floor. Skip practically fell out. "Message received. Thanks for the tip!"

The doors closed on four knowing smirks.

Skip trudged down the carpeted hallway muttering, "Damn," then louder, "Damn it," as he fished for keys that felt heavier than usual.

Inside his apartment, everything was too neat, museum neat. On the kitchen table lay Vic the Blade's abandoned duffel, unzipped and gutted like a fish. Gear everywhere: a remote-controlled reconnaissance robot the size of a football, coiled climbing rope, a dry-bag stuffed with scuba regs, a trauma kit that could stabilize a gunshot wound, and a laptop still in its sleeve.

The answering machine blinked red like an angry eye. Skip hit play while raiding the fridge for the last beer.

Vic's voice, tight with leftover terror: "I know I left the bag. Keep it. Burn it. I don't care. Just never call me again. And throw the damn thing away. I'm never going back there. Ever."

Beep.

Skip sank into a chair, cracked the beer, and stared at the little robot. Its camera eye stared back, black and unblinking. On impulse he flicked the remote. The bot whirred to life, treads humming, tiny antenna twitching like an insect.

He rolled it across the table, past the climbing gear, past the scuba mask, past the first-aid kit that suddenly looked a lot like preparation for something that bled.

Skip took a long pull from the bottle and watched the robot circle a coil of rope like a shark.

Somewhere across town, an old house waited, patient, amused, and very much awake.

The Robot

Eye That Looked Back

Tuesday morning on Mount Triplet Road, and the sun did its best to pretend everything was normal. Birds chirped. A sprinkler hissed across someone's perfect lawn. The house at number 32 squatted in silence, windows dark, waiting.

Across the street, Skip Hargrove sat in his parked sedan like a man waiting for a firing squad to finish their cigarettes. On the passenger seat: Vic the Blade's laptop, screen glowing, and the little recon robot's twin joysticks. A strip of black electrical tape held a cheap action-cam to the bot's back like a makeshift dorsal fin.

Skip flexed his fingers. "If I can't sell this place in person, I'll sell it online. Virtual tours are the future, baby."

He thumbed the sticks. Across the street, the robot rolled off the curb, treads crunching over fallen maple seeds, up the cracked cobblestone path, and miraculously, under the front door that opened just wide enough to admit it before closing again with the soft finality of a coffin lid.

Inside, the robot's camera swept the foyer, grainy but clear. Skip guided it past the staircase, into the living room where dust motes drifted like lazy galaxies. Kitchen next: yellowed linoleum, ancient Frigidaire, a single dead fly on the windowsill. Then the basement door creaked open by itself, inviting.

Down the wooden stairs it went, treads clacking.

Skip leaned closer to the screen. "Come on, safe, safe, safe—"

The basement appeared. There: the old iron safe beside the furnace, lid yawning open like it had been waiting for company. And beside it, a ragged hole in the concrete floor, big enough to swallow a man whole, edges blackened as if burned.

Standing between safe and hole was the old woman. Motionless. Head tilted, listening.

Skip's breath fogged the screen. "Cheese, you old bat."

The robot took one brave step forward and clipped an empty paint can. It rolled with a hollow clang that echoed like a dinner bell.

The old woman turned.

Skip's thumb stabbed the reverse button. Too late.

On-screen, her face filled the camera (close enough to count every liver spot, every broken capillary). She bent, picked up the fallen can… and looked straight into the lens.

Skip whispered, "You can't see it. You can't—"

A hand, pale, veined, impossibly long, pushed through the laptop screen like it was made of water. Knuckles like walnuts closed around Skip's throat.

He gagged, eyes bulging. The hand kept coming, elbow, forearm, the smell of earth and attic dust flooding the car.

A voice, dry as dead leaves: "Boo."

Witch-cackle laughter filled the sedan.

Skip slammed the laptop shut. The hand severed at the wrist, dissolving into black smoke that stank of mildew and old blood.

He stumbled out of the car, coughing, clawing at his neck. Across the street, on the second floor, lace curtains parted. The old woman stood in the window, smiling wide, waving like a grandmother on Easter Sunday.

Skip spun, still wheezing, just as a young mother strolled past pushing a stroller. The little girl from last night (pigtails, evil grin) walked beside her.

Skip pointed instinctively. "Quit hounding me, kid! I said I'll get the money!"

The child's face crumpled into theatrical tears. The mother whirled, furious.

"How dare you speak to my daughter like that, you creep!"

She snatched the girl's hand and stormed off. Over her shoulder, the child glanced back and gave Skip the universal two-fingered "I'm watching you" sign.

Skip rubbed the bruises blooming on his throat, muttering, "I need—"

A gust of wind whipped down the street, lifting a single sheet of newspaper. It slapped against Skip's shins and clung there like it had chosen him. The classifieds page. Bold red circle around one ad:

PARANORMAL INVESTIGATORS
"NO HAUNT TOO TOUGH"
24-HOUR EMERGENCY RESPONSE
WE GUARANTEE RESULTS
OR YOUR MONEY BACK!

Skip stared at the phone number until it burned into his retinas.

"—professionals," he finished, voice hoarse.

He looked back at the house. The old woman was still in the window, but now she pressed one palm against the glass and slowly, deliberately, drew a finger across her own throat.

Skip crumpled the newspaper page in his fist.

Tuesday had just gone from bad to biblical.

The Call

URGENT!

Looking for Ghost Exterminator! Must rid house of an old ghost. Pay BIG BUCKS for a fast job.

CALL NOW! KIL-GHOST

CALL NOW! DRY-SUSHI

Scratches, chips, or dull surface killing your hook? Fix it fast with pro-grade bowling ball repair kits — resurfacing pads, filler, polish & easy instructions included. Everything the serious bowler needs to restore that fresh-out-of-box reaction. Same-day shipping!

BOWLING BALL REPAIR KITS & CAREGIVER

NEED GRASS

GOLF COURSE GRADE LAWN!

Tired of a patchy yard? Get lush, golf course-grade grass delivered and installed this week — deep emerald, dense, weed-free turf that feels like putting green velvet underfoot. Limited stock, call GET-LAWN now for your free quote and turn your lawn into the envy of the neighborhood overnight.

CALL NOW! GO-GRASS

THUGS TERRIFY 2,500 IN THEATRE HOLD-UP

Eight Gunmen Raid Brooklyn Film House, Seize $2,500 and Shoot Way Out.

A POLICEMAN IS WOUNDED

Robber Also Believed Hit in Pistol Battle During Auto Chase—Car Is Found.

TRIP TO THE MOON!

TRIP TO THE MOON COMIC BOOK STORE

Call Goes Out

Newspaper Printing Plant
Midnight Shift

Deep beneath the city, in a cavernous warehouse that never sleeps, the great rotary presses roar like iron dragons. The air is thick with the hot-metal smell of fresh ink and the electric ozone of machinery running at redline. Conveyor belts hiss endlessly, feeding acres of newsprint into the maw of the machine. Overhead, fluorescent tubes buzz and flicker, throwing hard white light across the faces of men and women who have long since stopped noticing the noise.

A single sheet flashes past the observation window, caught for an instant in the strobing glare: a desperate block of red text screaming for attention among the obituaries and car dealership ads.

URGENT! Looking for ghost exterminator!
Must rid a house of an old ghost. Pay big
bucks for a fast job. Call now! KIL-GHOST.

The sheet vanishes into the collating blades. A thousand identical cries for help ride out on pallets, destined for every doorstep, diner counter, and laundromat in the metropolitan area before dawn.

A Dim Apartment
Lit Only by a Computer Screen

In a third-floor walk-up that smells of ramen and broken dreams, twenty-six-year-old Kyle "GhostBro96" Moretti sits hunched over his glowing monitor. The rest of the apartment is dark; he sold the lamps for rent money last month. Empty energy-drink cans form aluminum stalagmites around his chair. On-screen, Job List refreshes every three seconds like a heartbeat. When Skip's ad finally appears, bold and fresh and bleeding desperation, Kyle actually gasps. He leans so close his nose almost touches the glass. Fingers that haven't been steady since college fly across the keyboard. He copies the number, pastes it into his phone, and hesitates only long enough to whisper a prayer to whatever saint looks after unemployed paranormal Social Media Streamers.

The Unemployment Office
Mid-Morning

The waiting room is a fluorescent purgatory of cracked plastic chairs and the faint smell of despair. A line of tired souls snakes between velvet ropes while a wall-mounted television drones about weekend weather. Among them stands Dana Valdez, Channel 9's newest field reporter, clutching a dog-eared newspaper someone abandoned on the radiator. She's killing time before an interview with the director about "job-market trends." Boredom makes her flip to the classifieds. Her manicured nail stops on Skip's ad. She reads it once, twice, then a third time for the sheer glorious absurdity. A grin sharp enough to cut glass spreads across her face. She tears the ad out with a satisfying rip, stuffs it into her blazer pocket, and strides out past the security guard, already rehearsing voice-over lines about "the city's most haunted real-estate nightmare."

University Dorm
2:17 p.m.

Music thumps through the cinder-block walls of Hawthorne Hall, room 314. One half of the suite is a raging afternoon pre-game; the other half is sacred ground for the campus chapter of "Skeptical Inquirer Society—But Make It Fun." Three juniors—Owen Park, Mei-Ling Chen, and Darius Washington—sit cross-legged on the carpet surrounded by empty Red Bull cans and half-built electromagnetic field detectors made from disposable vape parts. A single fluorescent desk lamp illuminates the newspaper spread between them like a treasure map. When Mei-Ling's finger lands on the ad, the music across the room might as well disappear. Three pairs of eyes go wide. Owen actually squeals. High-fives turn into a three-way chest bump that knocks over a lava lamp. Within thirty seconds they're arguing over who gets to carry the proton-pack prototype they've been building for the senior prank.

Madame Zorina's Fortune & Reading Parlor
Late Afternoon

The little shop on Esoteric Row smells of sandalwood, rose attar, and secrets. Velvet drapes the color of dried blood keep out the afternoon sun. Madame Zorina—real name Ruth Kowalski, age somewhere between sixty-five and immortal—sits at a round table draped in midnight-blue cloth. A porcelain teacup steams beside a crystal ball that has never worked but looks fabulous. She turns the pages of the newspaper with the slow ceremony of a high priestess. When she reaches the classifieds, her penciled eyebrow climbs toward her turban. She sets the cup down with a delicate clink, draws a silver circle around the ad three times widdershins, and smiles the slow, satisfied smile of a woman who has waited seventy years for the universe to finally send her a worthy opponent.

Burger Palace off MLK Boulevard
11:43 p.m.

The fluorescent lights here are harsh and unforgiving, revealing every grease stain on the Formica. Three young men in thrift-store trench coats huddle in the corner booth like Cold War spies. Between them: one shared newspaper, three trays of fossilized fries, and the solemn remains of a twenty-piece nugget bucket. The tallest—goes by "Reverend" though no church ever ordained him—smooths the help-wanted section with reverent care. They read Skip's ad in hushed tones, the way monks once read forbidden manuscripts. Wallets come out. Pockets are turned inside out. The grand total: one dollar, two dimes, seven pennies, and a button from a coat that died in 1997. They stare at the pathetic pile, then at each other. Without a word they nod—grim, determined, broke, and absolutely certain this is their destiny. Reverend dips a fry in ketchup and circles the ad like he's signing a blood oath.

St. Agnes Rectory Office
Wednesday Morning

Sunlight pours through stained-glass windows, painting the threadbare carpet in jeweled colors. Father Michael O'Leary, eighty-three and still counting every penny like it's his last, sits at the roll-top desk with a green banker's visor perched on his bald head. Beside him, Father Daniel Park—thirty-two, newly ordained, and secretly terrified the world is bigger than seminary prepared him for—flips through yesterday's newspaper while the coffee brews. His finger freezes on the now-familiar block of red text. He nudges the old priest. Father Michael adjusts his bifocals, reads, and for the first time since Vatican II crosses himself twice in rapid succession. The collection plate suddenly feels very, very light.

Across the city, phones began to ring.

The Interviews

Parade of Hopefuls

Wednesday morning, and the cramped back office of Hargrove Realty smelled of burnt coffee, desperation, and the ghost of a thousand failed deals. A wobbly folding table and two plastic chairs served as Skip's throne room. A hand-scrawled sign taped to the door read:

The line already snaked down the hallway and out onto the sidewalk, a bizarre parade of the curious, the broke, and the borderline unhinged.

Skip sat hunched over a stack of crumpled résumés, eyes bloodshot, tie loosened like a noose he'd given up on. A half-empty bottle of antacids rattled every time he reached for it.

He cleared his throat. "Okay, people! Let's start this circus."

Interview #1
Dana Valdez, Channel 9 News

Dana strode in like she owned the building, blazer sharp enough to slice bread, cameraman trailing behind with a rig that probably cost more than Skip's car. She flashed the smile that had terrorized city-council members for three seasons.

Skip didn't bother standing. "So you want to film the ghost?"

"Exactly," Dana said, perching on the edge of the chair like a hawk. "We go in, lock off cameras, catch the old hag ripping faces or whatever she does. Overnight ratings gold."

"But you don't actually get rid of ghosts. You just record them screaming."

Dana's smile never wavered. "That's the beauty. We don't fix problems, we monetize them."

Skip rubbed his temples. "Tell me you didn't sleep your way into that anchor chair."

Her eyes turned to blue ice. "No, honey. I'm just a world-class bitch with cheekbones that open doors. So do I have the job or not?"

Skip leaned forward until they were nose to nose. "Lady, I need the ghost gone, not trending on Social Media."

He cupped hands to mouth. "Next!"

Dana stood, smoothing her skirt. "Your loss, Hargrove. When this story breaks, remember who offered you fifteen minutes of fame."

The cameraman nearly tripped over his own cables backing out.

Skip popped two antacids and muttered, "Lord, give me strength or give me bourbon."

The line shuffled forward. The circus was just getting started.

Interview #2
The Science Nerds
Who Never Watched the Movie

The door burst open and three lanky figures clanked in, moving like astronauts who'd built their suits out of RadioShack clearance and desperation. Owen, Mei-Ling and Darius, in wire-mesh jumpsuits were wrapped in Christmas-tree lights and duct tape. Tin-foil caps sprouted copper antennae. Each clutched a homemade cattle prod the size of a pool cue, wrapped in enough electrical tape to mummify a horse.

Skip stared, mouth half-open. "And you are…?"

In perfect unison, like they'd rehearsed in the hallway: "We are ghost exterminators."

Skip snorted. "For a second there I thought you were gonna say 'busters.'"

The leader, Owen, adjusted his name tag and foil crown. "No, sir. We don't bust ghosts. We exterminate them. Scientifically."

Skip leaned back, folding his arms. "Enlighten me, Bill Nye the Ghost-Slayer Guy."

Mei-Ling stepped forward, eyes shining behind safety goggles. "Ghosts are residual electromagnetic anomalies trapped in a quantum feedback loop. We've calculated the exact frequency—"

"—plus or minus twelve percent," Darius, added helpfully.

"—and these rods are tuned to deliver a counter-resonant pulse that will disrupt the entity's cohesion field and literally shock it out of the house."

Skip blinked. "You have no idea what you just said, do you?"

All three shook their heads in cheerful honesty.

"We found the suits and the notes in an old locker behind the physics lab," Owen admitted. "Some grad student vanished in '98. Figured he was onto something."

Skip looked them up and down, the blinking LEDs, the foil crackling with static, the fact that Darius's left prod was already smoking faintly.

"What's with the chain-mail onesies?"

"Faraday mesh," Mei-Ling said proudly. "When we zap the ghost, any retaliatory ectoplasmic discharge gets grounded through the suits. Ghost touches us—ghost gets zapped harder."

Owen held up a fourth suit, smaller, clearly meant for a willing real-estate agent. "We brought you one. One-size-fits-most."

Skip stared at the glittering silver jumpsuit like it was the One Ring.

He stood so fast the folding table rocked. "You're hired."

Then he threw the door wide and bellowed into the hallway: "Screw the rest of the interviews! You're all hired! Every single one of you lunatics! The TV chick too!"

A cheer went up from the corridor—part triumph, part terror.

Skip pointed at the students. "You three, front and center. You're my new best friends. Everybody else, we meet at the house tomorrow night. Bring holy water, EMF meters, cameras, sage, flamethrowers, whatever you've got. We're ending this."

He looked at the tin-foil trio, already vibrating with excitement.

"And for the love of God, somebody bring extra batteries."

Wednesday Noon
The Job

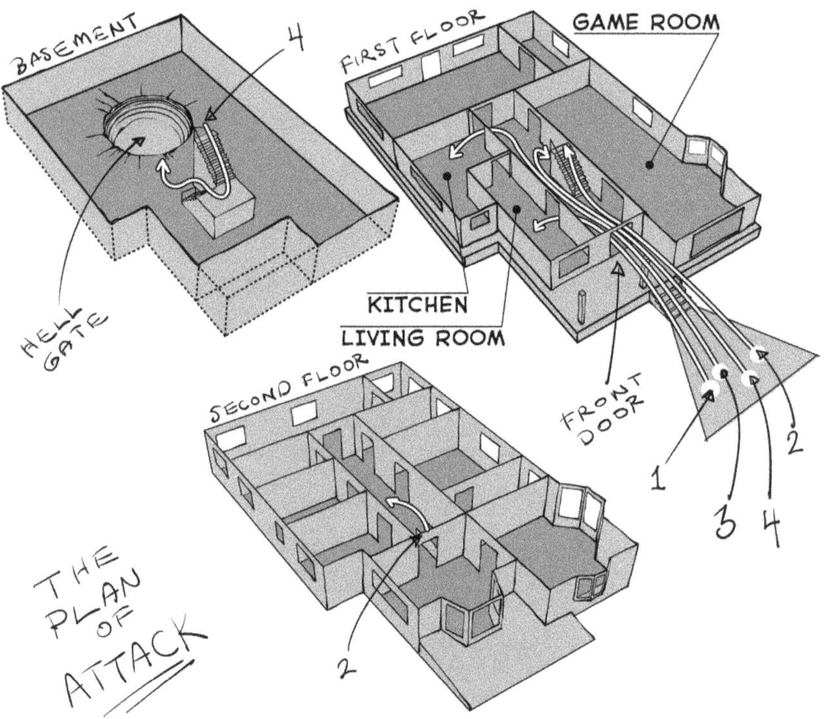

1. OUIJA BOARDERS
2. EXORCIST PRIESTS
3. POLTERGEIST SPECIALIST
4. STUDENTS

Army Arrives… and Departs

Wednesday noon, and the lawn of 32 Mount Triplet Road looked like Comic-Con had collided with a Renaissance fair and lost a fight with a church rummage sale.

Skip Hargrove stood at the end of the cobblestone walk in his borrowed Faraday-mesh jumpsuit, tin-foil hat crinkling every time he moved. Christmas lights blinked along his sleeves like a low-rent Iron Man. Around him clustered the strangest posse ever assembled: Dana Valdez and her Channel 9 crew with a camera the size of a bazooka; the three surviving university students clutching sparking cattle prods; Madame Zorina in full purple regalia, turban feathers trembling; the three broke-as-hell Ouija enthusiasts clutching their board like a holy relic; and two priests—one ancient, one terrified—clutching rosaries and a Super Soaker full of holy water.

Skip raised both arms like a deranged conductor. "This is the house. The ghost is mean, old, and ugly as sin. I want her gone. Today. Do this, and I double the money."

Across the street, the little girl in the faded sundress watched from the shade of a maple. She pointed two fingers at her eyes, then at Skip. Then drew one finger slow across her throat.

Skip swallowed hard. "Right. Go!"

They charged. Thirty people stormed the porch in a chaotic stampede of chanting, flashing lights, and one cameraman running backward while yelling "Keep it rolling!"

Inside, the house swallowed them whole.

Living Room

The Ouija boarders dropped to their knees around the coffee table like it was an altar. Two placed trembling fingers on the planchette while the third stood ready with a legal pad and a pen stolen from a bank.

"Spirit, why do you remain?"

Nothing.

"Spirit, speak to us!"

The planchette twitched, then shot across the board: H-E-S-T-O-L-E-M-Y-H-O-U-S-E

The third guy scribbled furiously.

"Anything else?"

The planchette zipped again: L-O-O-K-B-E-H-I-N-D-Y-O-U

They turned.

The darkness poured out of the basement doorway like living oil.

"Boo," it whispered, in the old woman's voice.

Basement

The three students formed a nervous triangle, prods raised. Their night-vision goggles painted everything sickly green.

"Final confrontation always happens in the basement," Mei-Ling declared.

A spitball of pure darkness hung in the center of the room—an impossible hole that drank light.

"Holy smokes, an inter-dimensional rift!"

Mei-Ling leaned over the edge. "Cover me, I'm gonna spit."

Two pale arms the size of bridge cables erupted from the pit and yanked her and Owen down without a sound.

Darius screamed, "Goose! Hicks!" and swung his prod like a Knight.

Dana Valdez appeared at the foot of the stairs, microphone first.

"Tell our viewers how you feel watching your friends get devoured by the black anus of evil!"

Darius tried to shove past her. The arms returned and dragged him under.

Dana spun to camera, unflappable. "Three brave students gave their lives today. Their sacrifice will not be—"

The darkness rose like a wave. The feed cut to static.

Second Floor Study

Fathers Michael and Daniel finished the last room, sprinkling holy water in graceful arcs.

"All done," the old priest sighed.

The hallway beyond the open door was absolute black—no light, no depth, just void.

Their candles should have cast at least a flicker.

Instead, the darkness puckered like lips and blew. Both flames died at once.

The priests crossed themselves in perfect, terrified synchronization.

Kitchen → Game Room

Madame Zorina moved through the rooms like a bloodhound, fingertips brushing counters, cabinets, the edge of the old pool table. With every touch, memories flared—ghost images of a young woman laughing, dancing, kissing a soldier goodbye at the door, rocking babies, growing old.

In the game room the memories stopped. The old woman stood waiting, solid and furious.

"You've lived a full life," Zorina said softly. "Why cling?"

"I have no choice."

The old woman seized Zorina's temples. The psychic's eyes rolled white as every memory of joy and grief poured into her like molten lead. She screamed once, a sound that cracked plaster, and the darkness drank her whole.

Skip watched it all on the laptop feed until the old woman's face filled the screen, grinning inches away. He slammed the lid, backed across the street—and tripped over the curb, landing hard on the cobblestones inside the property line.

He looked up. She was right there.

Her hand shot out, seized his jumpsuit—and blue-white lightning crackled. The mesh suit discharged a vicious arc. The old woman yelped and recoiled, smoking slightly.

"Ouch!"

Skip scrambled backward. Her arms stretched, then vanished at the wrists the moment they crossed the invisible boundary. She pulled back; hands reappeared. She tried again—same result.

Skip's eyes widened. "You're trapped! You can't leave the property!"

He actually laughed, a cracked, desperate sound.

She snatched a fallen branch and whipped him across the shins until it snapped.

Skip hopped, cursing, then remembered the spare vial of holy water in his pocket. He uncorked it with his teeth and flung the contents.

The old woman threw her arms up theatrically. "I'm melting! Melting!"

She dropped to her knees, wailing—then straightened, perfectly fine, and smirked.

"You need a reservoir to even catch my attention, boy."

Skip's bravado drained away.

"You stole my house to pay a gambling debt."

"You were dying!" Skip yelled back.

"It was my house. My memories. My family—however distant my niece and her lazy surfer son, Adam—were supposed to have it. Not the city! Not you!"

Skip threw up his hands. "Fine! I'll just not pay the debt. Let them kill me. At least it'll be quick."

She smiled, sweet and terrible. "Then you come straight to me. No pearly gates for thieves, Skippy."

A passing old man walking his terrier chuckled. "Sucks to be you, dude."

Skip glared at the empty air where she'd stood. She was gone, but her whisper rode the wind.

"Die."

Skip stood alone on the cobblestones, foil hat askew, jumpsuit scorched, staring at a house that now contained the shredded remains of every expert he'd hired.

Somewhere inside, something ancient and patient began to laugh.

Thursday Morning
The Realesternator
11—1

Realestaternator

Thursday morning, and the house at 32 Mount Triplet Road looked like it had lost a fight with a cathedral. Rain, holy, blessed, and delivered by a rented tanker truck, sheeted off the roof in silver curtains. Every window wept. The lawn was a lake.

In the basement, the old woman stood at the edge of the impossible pit, listening to the distant, a chorus of screams rising from the fiery glow below. A satisfied smile played on her lips.

A soft whisper drifted up from the depths.

"Come…"

Then—creak—the front door.

She was darkness before her feet hit the first stair.

First Floor Lobby

A new robot, armored in duct tape and righteous purpose, rolled in. On its back: a cellphone duct-taped to a Super Soaker loaded with Vatican-grade holy water. The nozzle swiveled like a tank turret.

The darkness hesitated.

The robot opened fire.

A pressurized jet of sanctified H_2O hosed the lobby. Darkness shrieked and retreated into the living room, steaming like dry ice.

The front door swung wide. Skip Hargrove strode in wearing the spare Faraday suit, battle-scarred and blinking weakly, electric cattle prod crackling in one hand, water cannon in the other.

"Call me the Realestaternator."

The darkness lunged. Lightning crawled over Skip's suit; the entity recoiled, resolving into the old woman clutching scorched hands.

"Yeah," Skip said, advancing, "time to pack up, grandma."

He jabbed the prod. Blue arcs danced. She screamed and vanished.

Skip ripped the cannon off the robot and charged the stairs, spraying like a one-man exorcism.

Second Floor

Room by room he went—bedrooms, bathroom, closets—holy water sloshing in wide arcs. In the master bath he caught her reflection charging in the mirror. She touched his image; the suit discharged with a thunder-crack. She reappeared on her knees, palms smoking.

"Glutton for punishment?" Skip asked pleasantly, and hosed her down again.

She vanished.

Skip slapped open his laptop. Downstairs, the camera-bot rolled obediently.

Basement Feed

The old woman materialized, rubbing a freshly burned arm. She punted the robot so hard it spun like a top.

Skip's voice echoed from upstairs: "Second floor's baptized, sweetheart. Guess where I'm headed next?"

First Floor

Knives flew like angry hornets. Skip ducked behind the sofa as steel thunked into upholstery. He blind-fired holy water around the edge, rolled, came up shooting.

The kitchen knives clattered uselessly to the wet floor.

Library – Last Stand

Rain hammered the windows. Skip stepped in, cannon raised.

"Last room on this floor. Shame about the first editions."

"You monster!" the old woman snarled.

"Me? You murdered a dozen people yesterday."

She gestured proudly at the shelves. "My husband collected these. He read them all. They… awakened him."

Skip's gaze slid across the spines:

How to Kill, What It Takes, Faces of Death, Keeping Them Alive, To Serve Man, Eating for Survival…

His face went slack. "You two were—"

"Doctors?" She looked almost offended. "No, you idiot. My husband is a hunter. People. For sport."

"Yeah," Skip muttered, "that was my next guess."

The old man materialized behind him (tall, gaunt, eyes like frozen ponds). He seized Skip's suit and howled as current cooked his palms. Skip fired the last of the cannon; the ghost dodged.

Battery indicator blinked red—eight percent.

Skip smashed a window with the prod. Rain, blessed, endless rain, poured in.

"That's not rain," the old woman hissed.

"Nope. Tanker truck. Your idea, actually."

The darkness boiled into the room, hungry.

Skip dove head-first through the broken window.

Side Lawn

He landed hard in the mud. The truck operator spun the nozzle, blasting the side of the house like a firehose on Judgment Day.

Skip rolled, came up running. The old man was already on the porch, coat flapping like raven wings.

Skip hit the sidewalk boundary and spun. "Hose me!"

The operator grinned. "You're the boss."

A wall of water slammed into Skip and the old man both. The ghost shrieked, skin blistering, and flung Skip away like a rag doll.

Skip crawled the last foot to safety, rolled onto his back, gasping.

The little girl skipped up, pig-tails bouncing.

"Message from the boss," she chirped. "It's Thursday. Quit screwing around and sell the house. They're just dead people. Get rid of them."

She waved. "Toodles!"

Skip staggered upright, dripping, and walked the property line until he faced the old man.

"Hey. Tall, dark, and murderous."

The old man raised one eyebrow.

Skip crooked a finger. "Come here."

The ghost stepped forward, hand reaching. Fingers vanished at the invisible wall.

Skip smirked. "Offer you can't refuse. You and your lovely bride vacate —permanently— or I come back with an army of tanker trucks, priests, and every volt the city can spare. We turn this place into the world's holiest car-wash until there's nothing left of you but steam."

He checked his watch. "Thirty seconds."

The old man stared — then simply wasn't there.

Skip cupped hands to mouth. "Is that a yes or a no?"

Only the rain answered, drumming on the roof like a thousand impatient fingers.

Skip looked at the house — soaked, steaming, suddenly very, very quiet.

He exhaled a laugh that sounded almost like hope.

Thursday Evening
The Deal

Dead Decide to Live Again
Basement – Thursday Afternoon

The pit in the center of the concrete floor glowed a dull, angry red, like the eye of something ancient and impatient. The old woman stood at its edge, arms folded, watching flames lick upward. Her husband materialized beside her in a swirl of cold air that smelled of earth and old blood.

"Didn't go well?" she asked without looking over.

"He's a real bugger," the old man muttered, flexing fingers that still sparked faintly from the Faraday suit. "Like trying to scare a Wall Street banker. Only thing that frightens trash like him is losing money. Everything else? Fluff."

A low, hungry whisper rose from the pit.

"Come to me…"

The old woman shivered. "They're calling again."

Her husband stared into the glow, face grim. "Technology's finally caught up. Holy-water tanker trucks. Electric ghost prods. We're dead, love—proper dead—and still losing."

She gave a dry, papery laugh. "We might as well be alive. We'd stand a better chance."

The old man froze. Then snapped his fingers so hard the sound cracked like a gunshot.

"Alive," he repeated, eyes lighting with predatory delight. "And no longer bound to this cursed patch of dirt."

Hell – Same Moment

An abysmal cavern the size of a cathedral, walls weeping liquid fire. Rivers of lava hissed and popped. Screams rose and fell like a demonic orchestra warming up.

Behind a jagged boulder, Dana Valdez crouched in tattered blazer and one heel, mascara streaked like war paint. Shadowy things with too many teeth zipped past, giggling.

Everything went suddenly, unnaturally quiet.

Dana risked a peek.

The old woman sprinted straight at her, arms outstretched.

Dana screamed and squeezed her eyes shut.

Basement – Instant Later

A manicured hand shot out of the pit, nails still perfect, and clawed at the concrete rim.

"Hold on, I got you!"

Owen, foil hat askew but very much alive—grabbed the wrist and hauled. Dana came up gasping, soaked in sweat and brimstone, but solid. Real. Breathing.

She sucked in air like it was champagne. "That tastes like a tall glass of lemonade on a summer porch."

"Welcome back to the living," Owen said, grinning like a madman.

Dana looked around at the basement, then down at her own body—flesh, blood, heartbeat thundering in her ears. She cupped her breasts experimentally. "Firm. Very firm."

"Not much of a welcome if we're still trapped on the grounds," she added, voice already sharpening into reporter mode.

"Been there, done that," Owen said. "I've crossed the street and come back. Boundary's gone. We're free."

Dana's eyes narrowed. "And where exactly are we going?"

Owen pulled a soggy business card from his pocket—Skip's card, still readable.

"We," he said, tapping it, "are paying a house call to Skippy. His place. His rules. Our turn."

Dana's smile could have cut diamonds. "Ballsy move, honey."

She grabbed Owen by the collar and kissed him hard—victory, revenge, and something hungrier all at once.

From the depths of the pit, something ancient growled in frustration.

Upstairs, the old couple laughed—a sound like dry leaves scraping across a coffin lid.

The dead had decided to come back.

And they were bringing friends.

The Business

Advantage

Thursday evening, and the back office of Hargrove Realty had become a war room that smelled of gunpowder, powdered sugar, and cheap coffee.

The remaining Vipers, Lefty now wearing the invisible crown, Numbers, Smokes, and Porkchop, clustered around the water cooler like it was the last oasis on Earth. A box of day-old doughnuts bled custard onto a folding table.

Porkchop held up a glazed ring solemnly. "Normal vibe from a person? This size."

He spread his arms wide. "Vibe from that house right now? Twenty-five-foot doughnut. Animals are losing their minds for three blocks."

Lefty and Skip walked up, Lefty still combing his hair with the switchblade comb out of pure habit.

Lefty eyed Skip. "You're either brave or stupid walking back into Viper territory, suit."

Skip shrugged. "We've got a common enemy. Payback tastes better with friends."

Smokes nudged Porkchop. "Tell him the doughnut thing."

Lefty raised an eyebrow. "What about the doughnut?"

Before anyone could answer, the door opened.

Every Viper drew steel in one smooth motion.

Owen and Dana Valdez stepped inside, hands high, looking freshly resurrected and twice as pissed.

Numbers lowered his pistol a fraction. "Who the hell—"

Skip shoved past the guns and crushed both returnees in a bear hug. "You're alive!"

He dragged them to the sagging sofa like a man greeting prodigals. "Water! Somebody get them water!"

Lefty nodded. Numbers filled two paper cups.

Skip's voice dropped. "What do you remember?"

Dana shook her head. "Nothing. One second we're in the house, next we're on the lawn."

Owen drank greedily. Dana raised her cup—Skip's hand shot out and stopped her wrist.

"You sure about that?" he asked softly.

Owen convulsed. Darkness poured from his mouth like black smoke given claws. Smokes vanished inside it for a heartbeat, then the cloud spat him out, groaning.

Skip was already up, holy-water Super Soaker raised. "Everybody—cover!"

Every Viper produced brightly colored plastic water pistols like it was the most natural thing in the world. A rainbow of sanctified death sprayed across the office.

The darkness dove into Numbers. A heartbeat of silence.

Lefty whispered, "Numbers?"

Numbers turned, eyes solid black, voice a gravel whisper: "He wasn't thirsty."

He raised his real pistol and opened fire.

The office exploded into chaos—real bullets, holy water, and flying doughnuts. Lefty unloaded an entire magazine into the water cooler. It burst like a holy grenade, drenching Numbers from head to toe.

The darkness shrieked out of him, twisting, shrinking, until the last drop of blessed water turned it into harmless mist that evaporated with a hiss.

Silence.

Porkchop sniffed the air. "Vibe's gone. Like, really gone."

Smokes handed Numbers a fresh cup. "Drink, man."

Numbers drained it gratefully.

Lefty looked around at the bullet-riddled walls. "Cops are definitely coming."

Skip smiled. "Soundproof walls. Dance club next door. Relax."

He turned to Dana, who sat very still on the sofa, watching him with old, old eyes.

"How'd you know?" she asked in the old woman's voice.

Skip spun his laptop. Hit play.

Security footage from the house: Dana and Owen making out like the world was ending, clothes half-off, completely unaware of the robot filming from the mantel.

Skip whistled. "You two really go at it. My buddies here uploaded the director's cut to a pay site. Ten times what I owe the boss. We're square. Any profit left? These gentlemen keep it."

Dana looked at the circle of water guns pointed at her chest.

"You bastard," she hissed.

Skip bowed. "Realestaternator."

He sat beside her, casual as Sunday brunch.

"Now, Granny," he said gently, "tell me about the hole in the basement."

Aftermath
Heritage Haunted House
(Open for Business)

One Week Later – Basement

The pit that once breathed fire now sat quiet under a thick, church-blessed glass dome the size of a carnival booth. Gold lettering on the glass read:

OFFICIALLY SANCTIFIED BY THE ARCHDIOCESE OF THE CITY
(DO NOT TAP – SOULS MAY BITE)

Six coin-operated scenic binoculars ringed the dome like sentries. Down below, the glow had dimmed to a moody red night-light, just enough to make out vague shapes moving, tourist-friendly, not terrifying.

Numbers and Smokes swept the last of the plaster dust into neat piles.

Numbers whistled. "We are gonna be filthy rich."

Smokes flicked ash from an unlit cigarette. "Word."

Front Lawn – Same Day

Sunshine, fresh paint, and the smell of cut grass. The house looked almost respectable. Porkchop power-washed the porch while Lefty hung a new hand-painted banner:

HERITAGE HAUNTED HOUSE – EST. 1871
REAL HELL GATE INCLUDED.

Skip hammered the final stake into the lawn sign:

HERITAGE HAUNTED HOUSE
COME SEE AN AUTHENTIC CENTURY-OLD HOME
A GENUINE VIEW INTO THE AFTERLIFE!
100 % OF PROCEEDS BENEFIT
GAMBLING-ADDICTION RECOVERY PROGRAMS

The little girl watched from the sidewalk, arms crossed, looking severely disappointed in humanity.

"Are you serious?" she asked.

Skip wiped sweat from his brow and grinned the grin of a man who'd finally beaten the house. "Dead serious. Straight and narrow from here on out. Honest work, honest taxes, the whole bit."

She shrugged. "If you ever need another loan, my baby brother gives excellent rates."

"I'm good never owing your family again, thanks."

"Toodles!" She skipped away, pigtails bouncing like judgment itself.

A Channel 9 news van screeched to the curb. Dana Valdez stepped out in a crisp red blazer, looking ten years younger and twice as dangerous. She waved her crew into position, then crossed the street toward Skip.

"How's the old gang?" Skip asked.

"Priests are back saying Mass. Geeks are writing a paper nobody will believe. Ouija kids started a podcast. Everybody's alive, everybody remembers. Hell of a field trip."

Skip chuckled. "Hell. Good one."

Dana rolled her eyes. "It was meant to be."

He leaned on the signpost. "Always wondered—why'd you let the Vipers walk but send everyone else downstairs for snacks?"

Dana—or the thing wearing Dana like a tailored suit—gave a tired smile. "I had an abusive husband. I scared people, I let them go. When he scared people, he sent them below. Old marital habits." She shrugged. "He started sweet, ended monstrous. Sound familiar?"

Skip glanced at the dome. "That really Hell down there?"

"More like Purgatory's lobby. Every so often a demon pops up for takeout. We got everybody out before the main course."

A comfortable silence settled.

Skip nudged her shoulder. "So… second chance at life. Wanna come up and see me sometime?"

Dana smirked, tapped her stomach lightly. "Taken."

Skip followed her gaze across the street. Owen was hauling cables for the news crew, shirt off, grinning like he'd won the cosmic lottery.

"You gotta be kidding me."

"Nope. Hired him as my 'intern.' Among other duties." She patted the barely-there bump under her blazer. "He's twenty-five, studley, and mine."

Skip barked a laugh. "Scandalous doesn't cover it. Coffee, boyfriend, and a bun in the oven, all in one merger."

Dana gave him a wink sharp enough to draw blood. "Some of us know how to close a deal."

Behind them, the first tourists were already lining up, quarters glittering in their palms.

Skip looked at the house (his house now, legally and forever), at the dome glowing softly in the basement window, at the sign promising redemption in ten-minute intervals.

For the first time in years, Skip Hargrove felt something dangerously close to peace.

He adjusted the new name tag on his chest—TOUR GUIDE— and called to the gathering crowd.

"Step right up, folks! One genuine Heritage Haunted House, now with 100 % less eternal damnation and 100 % more charitable giving!"

Somewhere below, something ancient sighed, rolled over, and— for the moment—went back to sleep.

Skip grinned at the sky.

"House always wins," he said. "But this time, the house is mine."

Epilogue

OFFICIALLY SANCTIFIED BY
THE ARCHDIOCESE OF THE CITY
DO NOT TAP — SOULS MAY BITE

Six Months Later
America's Favorite Haunted House

Basement – Peak Tourist Season

The dome over the hell-gate gleamed under new LED spotlights. A velvet rope kept the line orderly. Six coin-operated binoculars clicked and whirred like hungry insects.

Father Michael, retired from active exorcism, now on salary, stood at a small podium beside the three original Ouija boarders, who had upgraded to matching HHH polo shirts.

Father Michael pointed with a laser pointer. "If you'll direct your attention to the flaming rock at eleven o'clock, that is the River of Sorrows. Juvenile imps often bathe there to rinse ash from their wings. Perfectly harmless… from this side of the glass."

A collective "ooh" rippled through the viewers.

A teenage girl squealed, "That little demon is totally waving at us!"

Ouija Border #1 leaned in smoothly. "He's saying he'd love to come upstairs and wear your intestines as a jump rope."

The girl squealed louder, delighted. "Can I take a picture?"

Numbers appeared like a benevolent ghost in a waistcoat. "No flash photography, please—spooks the locals. But we have 8410 glossies upstairs for only twenty dollars. Autographed by the imp on request."

Channel 9 Special Report – "I Survived 32 Mount Triplet Road"

Dana Valdez, now anchor of the prime-time slot and visibly pregnant, sat across from a parade of former "victims."

The Indian Father

"Yeah, the ghost had huge ugly eyes. I grabbed a lamp, held her off while my family escaped."

Dana, deadpan: "I heard your wife threatened to stop cooking if you bought the place."

He shifted. "Well… yes, but ultimately it was my decision."

Vic the Blade, still in sunglasses indoors

"I had a run-in with the (bleep). Would've (bleep) her silly if I didn't have a prior engagement."

Dana: "Sources say she nearly choked you to death."

Vic cleared his throat with macho dignity. "I employed advanced tactical disengagement. The, uh, flowerpot incident was unrelated."

The Newlywed Bride

"She was old and prunish—like the Wicked Witch, but worse."

Dana: "Pumpkinhead?"

"No, Wizard of Oz."

The Newlywed Groom, red-faced

"Guts everywhere. I fought her off so my wife could escape."

Dana, grinning: "I heard the ghost was young, naked, and in the shower with you."

He opened his mouth.

His wife cut in sharply: "He put his life on the line!"

Dana: "By staying behind while you ran screaming?"

The bride snatched the mic. "Details!"

The Indian Mother, eyes blazing

"That real-estate agent is a very bad man. The ghost told me everything."

Dana tried to move on.

The mother seized the microphone like it owed her money. "He has kinky sex with musical instruments! One time at band camp he—"

Dana yelled off-camera: "Cut! Cut! We're live, people!"

The screen smashed to a hastily prepared graphic:

TECHNICAL DIFFICULTIES
PLEASE ENJOY THIS PICTURE OF A KITTEN.

There was no kitten. Just text to add to the audience annoyance.

Somewhere in the background, Skip's laughter echoed over the airwaves, warm, rich, and finally, mercifully, debt-free.

The Heritage Haunted House was open 362 days a year, closed Good Friday and Christmas, out of respect.

And business had never been better.

The story continues in these books...

...on sale now from CriticalBlast•com

CriticalBlast•com